QUEEN OF THE KUIPER BELT

First edition paperback
ISBN 978-1-915579-33-1

Queen of the Kuiper Belt
Illustrations © David Hutchison. 2025

Music: The Split Rock © Joan Hutchison. 2015
Music: Nigel © Joan Hutchison. 2015
originally published in The Golden Grain

www.davidhutchison.info/theprospectors.html

Queen of the Kuiper Belt

Prospectors Book 2

David Hutchison

Ahab and Gert are playing cat snap.

There is a lurch. Alarms go off. The Ariselle is trapped in something.

A space spider has caught the Ariselle in its web.

They blast through the web. The space spider chases after them. They speed through space. Eventually the space spider gives up.

The fuel is almost out.
Gert: "Pluto is the nearest place to refuel."

A while later they arrive at dwarf planet Pluto.
Gert: "We don't have enough money. How are we going to buy fuel?"
Ahab holds up a phial of the youth generating green goo.
Ahab: "Perhaps we can sell the last one of these?"

They dock at the domed Clyde City.

Ahab: "How will it cost much to refuel our spaceship?"
Receptionist: "200 credits."
Ahab: "Do you want to buy youth generating goo?"
Receptionist: "I'm a robot. Youth generating goo is of no use to me."

Gert: "We'll have to try selling the goo somewhere else."
Ahab and Gert walk into the city.

CLYDE CITY

Ahab:"Rejuvenating goo for sale!"
People just walk past and ignore them.

The lads walk further into the city. They come across The Pluto Prairie Club; displaying a sign for a competition.

They spend the last of their money on the entrance fee.
Gert: "Do you have any musical instruments that I can borrow?"
Cashier: "Someone left this accordion."

There is already an act on the stage. Bert on his fiddle, playing the tune "The Split Rock" and his pet wolf Wolfie jumping through a hoop.

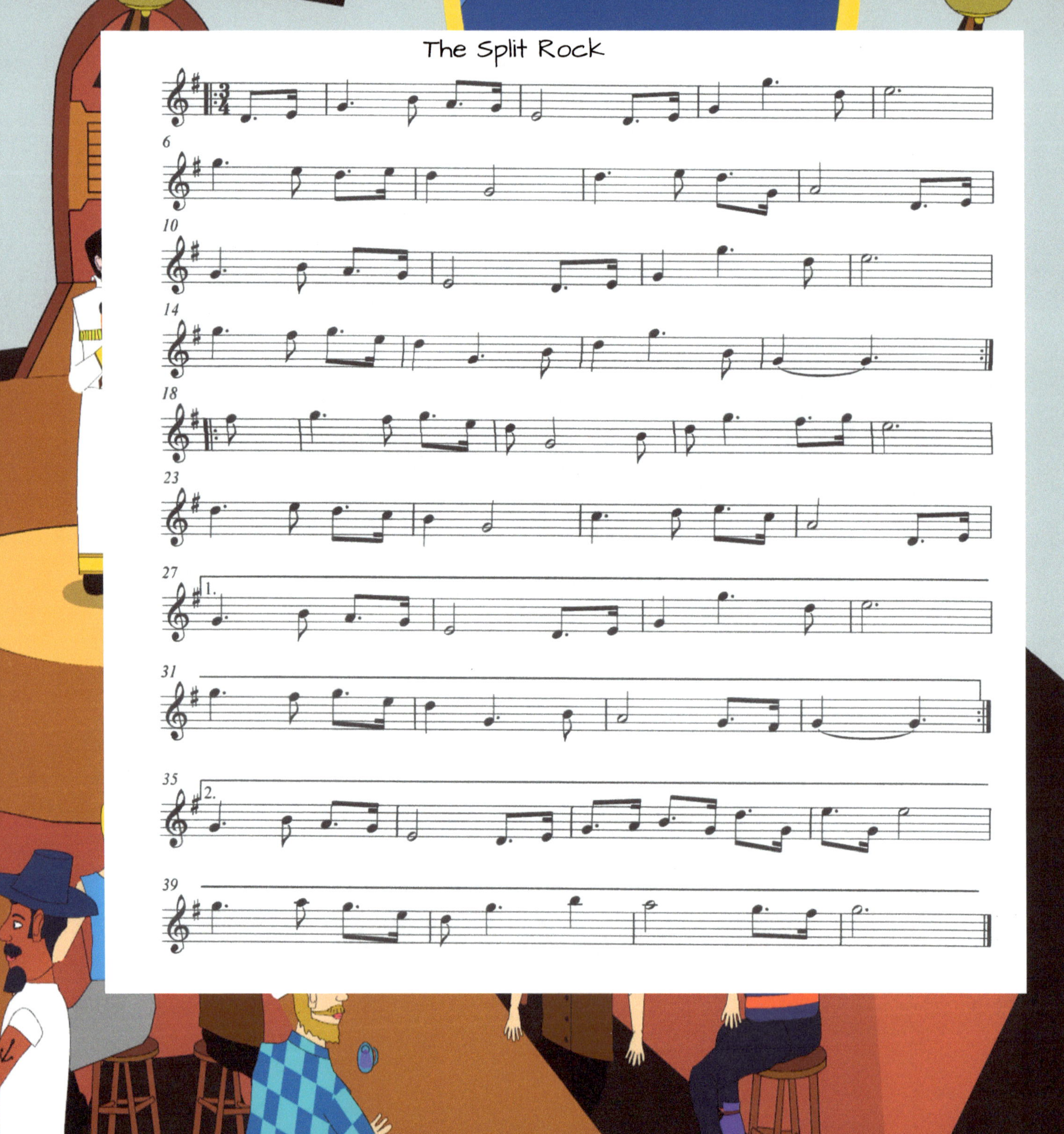

The Split Rock

Compère: "Thank you Bert & Wolfie. Now put your limbs together for Tentacle Tina."

Tentacle Tina comes through the saloon doors and up to the microphone. She plays a banjo tune called "Nigel".

The audience clap enthusiastically when Tentacle Tina finishes.

Compère: "And now we have Ahab and Gert."
Ahab: "Queen of the Kuiper Belt is about our cat Pip Pop."

Queen of the Kuiper Belt.

She's long and furry and grey.
She lies in the starlight all day.
Her skin is as velvet as felt.
She's the queen of the Kuiper Belt.
If a mouse runs past her at dawn
She looks down and stretches and yawns,
Her skin is as velvet as felt.
She's the queen of the Kuiper Belt.
In the far reaches of space
She licks her paws with grace,
Her skin is as velvet as felt.
She's the queen of the Kuiper Belt.

Compère: "Thank you Ahab and Bert. So now to the scores. In third place is Bert & Wolfie. In second place is Tentacle Tina."
Ahab and Gert hope that they will win.

Compère: "In first place is Sunny Bean."
Sunny Bean comes rushing through the saloon doors and onto the stage."
Sunny Bean:"Thank you everyone."

Gert: "It's her. Maybe she'll swap the prize money for some goo?"
Ahab: "Yes. Let's wait outside for her."

Sunny Bean: "I thought I recognised you two."
Ahab: "We need to refuel. Do you want to buy goo?"

Sunny Bean swaps her prize money for a phial of goo.
Ahab: "That's the last of it."

She rubs the goo on her face.

She waits for the wrinkles to fade.
Sunny Bean: "I need more goo!"

Ahab and Gert are having the Ariselle refuelled.
Sunny Bean sneaks up behind them.

Sunny Bean steps up into the Ariselle.

Sunny Bean chases after Pip Pop.

Sunny catches Pip Pop and carries her off in a bag.

Gert and Ahab find a ransom note left by Sunny Bean.
Ahab: "She's kidnapped Pip Pop. She wants more goo, but we don't have any left."

Ahab: "Poor Pip Pop."
Gert: "I've an idea. Do you have an empty phial?"
Ahab: "Yes, here you go."

Gert sneezes and fills up the phial with snot.
Ahab: "Hopefully it will fool her."

Ahab and Gert go back into the city. They find Sunny waiting near the club, carrying a wriggling sack.

Ahab hands the phial over. Gert takes Pip Pop out of the sack and gives her a cuddle. They head back to the Ariselle.

Sunny smears the goo under her sagging chin.
The wrinkles don't go away.
Sunny: "I've been tricked!"

The Ariselle blasts off into space.

Gert:" Maybe we should dress Pip Pop in a tutu
and get her to jump through a hoop?"
Ahab: "Ah like Bert and Wolfie!"
The Queen of the Kuiper Belt is not amused!